A TALE OF TWO CATS

WRITTEN BY
AYIN HILLEL

DRAWN BY
SHIMRIT ELKANATI

FANTAGRAPHICS BOOKS

Once upon a time there were two cats.

One black as tar,

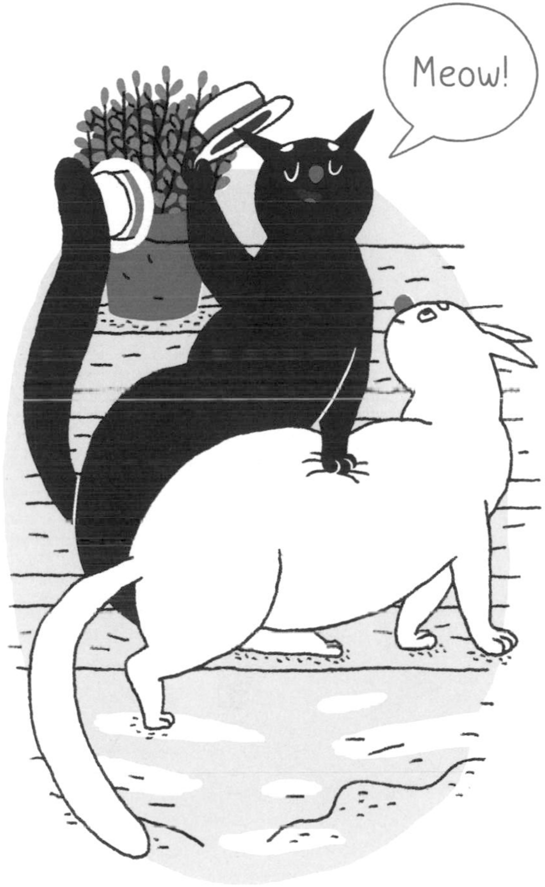
Meow!

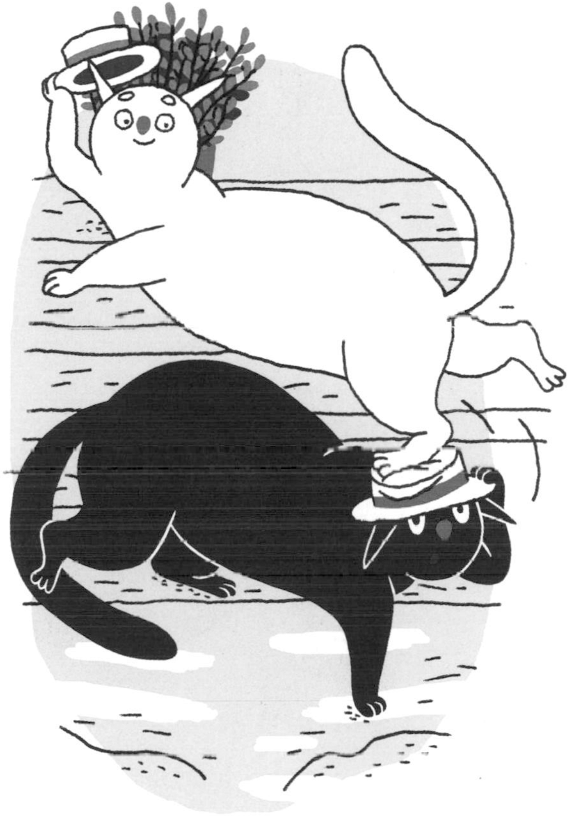

One white as whitewash.

Said the first cat, black as tar:
"I'm the prettiest by far."

Said the white one in reply:
"I'm lovelier. Need you ask why?"

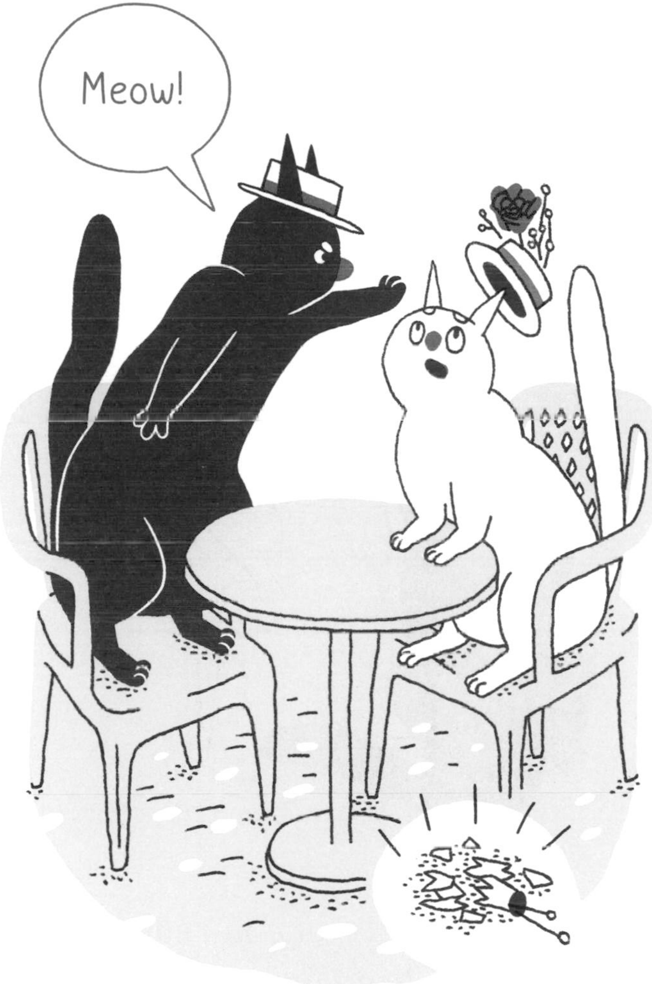
Meow!

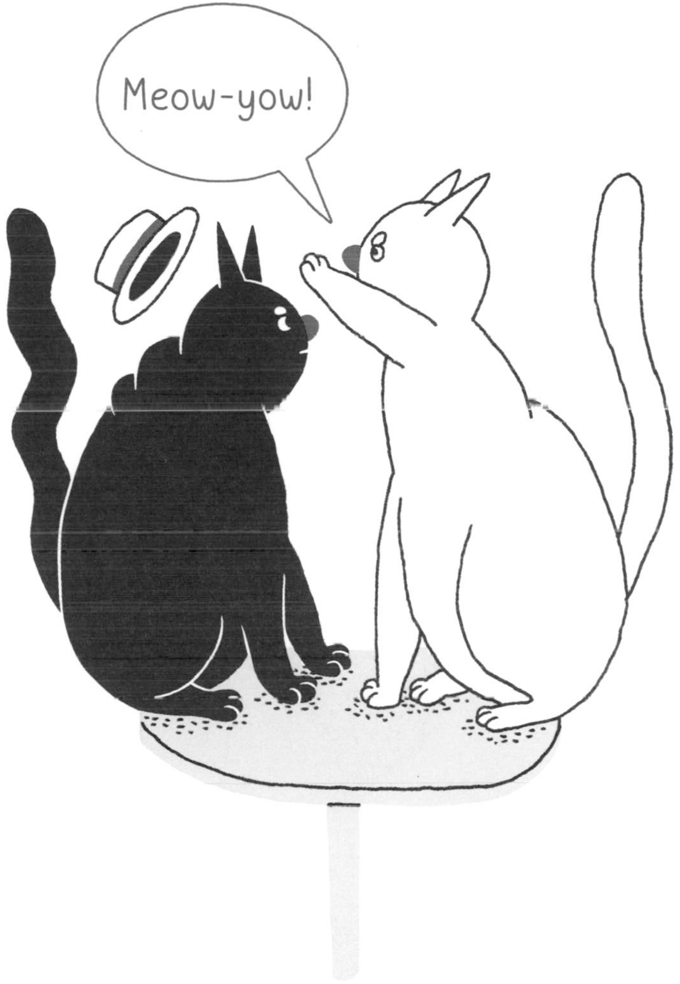
Meow-yow!

The black-as-tar cat was insulted.   The white-as-whitewash slighted, too.

With bristled fur, tails in the air,
They gave each other icy stares.

So black-as-tar and white-as-whitewash
Parted ways to pout and brood.

It was a rather nasty spat,

8

For each was quite a stubborn cat.

The day went by and one night passed,

Until they were fed up at last.

The black-as-tar cat
wondered:

"Perhaps my friend
the whitewash cat
is truly prettier than me?"

And white-as-whitewash
wondered:

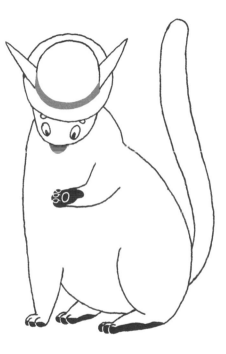

"Perhaps my friend
the tar-black cat
is the loveliest indeed?"

What did the black-as-tar cat do?
He jumped into a whitewash can.

What did the
white-as-whitewash cat do?
He jumped into a barrel of tar.

14

The black cat came out
white-as-whitewash.

The white cat came out
black-as-tar.

The black cat whitewashed,
The white cat tarred black —

All topsy-turvy
was the world!

They didn't know now who was who.
Just who was who, and what was what.

What distress, oh what a mess!
Meow! Meow! Meow!

"Meow!"
Whined the now-black cat,
"This tar's so itchy, sticky."

"Meow!"
Whined the now-white cat,
"This whitewash stings and clings."

"Meow-ow! Ow-ow!"
Whined the two.

So what did they do?
Hop, skip, one and two —

They raced each other to the sea,
And washed themselves all clean with glee.

They splashed and scrubbed
their fur and skin,
From head to toe, from tail to chin.

Then they came out from the sea,
Feeling quite stupendously.

Here the two cats are once more,
Nicer than they were before.

White as whitewash, black-as-tar,
More merry than before, by far.

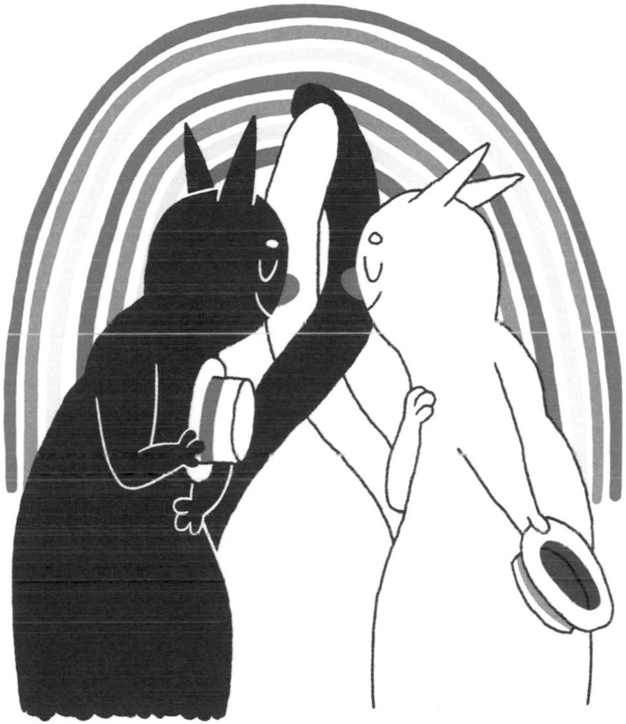

With their tails snuggled together,
They asked forgiveness from each other.

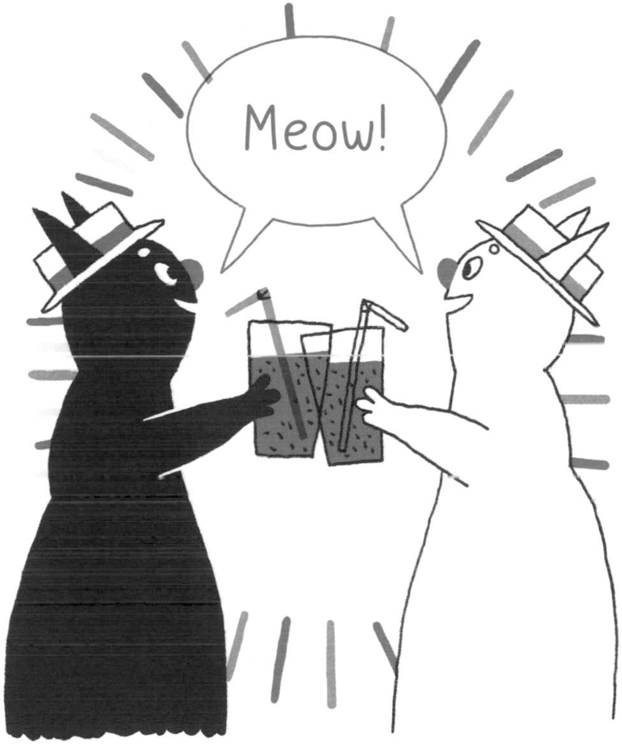
Meow!

"When we're not just one, but two —
We are lovely, me and you."

"And now, no matter what the weather,
We'll be best of friends forever!"

And off they rode to join the fun,
In the bus with everyone.

Translator: Ilana Kurshan
Editors: Conrad Groth, Rutu Modan, Yirmi Pinkus
Designer: Jacob Covey
Supervising Editor: Gary Groth
Production: Paul Baresh
Associate Publisher: Eric Reynolds
Publisher: Gary Groth

Fantagraphics Books, Inc.
7563 Lake City Way NE
Seattle, WA 98115

ISBN: 978-1-68396-266-3
First Fantagraphics Books edition: September 2019
Printed in Malaysia